Q & RAY

·CASE #3·
FOUL PLAY AT ELM TREE PARK

TRISHA SPEED SHASKAN

ILLUSTRATED BY STEPHEN SHASKAN

Graphic Universe™ • Minneapolis

For my brother, Jesse, for taking me out to
the ball game and being an all-time great.
Love you! —TSS

To Greg Hunter and Emily Harris, for believing
in this series and helping make it the best it
could be —SS

Graphic Universe™
A division of Lerner Publishing Group, Inc.
241 First Avenue North
Minneapolis, MN 55401 USA

For reading levels and more information, look up this title at www.lernerbooks.com.

Main body text set in CCDaveGibbonsLower 11.5/13.25.
Typeface provided by ComicCraft.

Library of Congress Cataloging-in-Publication Data

Names: Shaskan, Trisha Speed, 1973– author. | Shaskan, Stephen, illustrator.
Title: Foul play at Elm Tree Park / written by Trisha Speed Shaskan ; illustrated by Stephen
   Shaskan.
Description: Minneapolis : Graphic Universe, [2018] | Series: Q & Ray ; case #3 | Summary:
   Hedgehog Quillan Hedgson, a.k.a Q, and rat Ray Ratzberg are second-grade students and
   sleuths who use handwriting analysis and photographic evidence to solve the case of a stolen
   autographed baseball. | Description based on print version record and CIP data provided by
   publisher; resource not viewed.
Identifiers: LCCN 2017044293 (print) | LCCN 2017058393 (ebook) | ISBN 9781541523784 (eb pdf)
   | ISBN 9781512411492 (lb : alk. paper) | ISBN 9781541526440 (pb : alk. paper)
Subjects: LCSH: Graphic novels. | CYAC: Graphic novels. | Mystery and detective stories. |
   Stealing–Fiction. | Penmanship–Fiction. | Hedgehogs–Fiction. | Rats–Fiction.
Classification: LCC PZ7.7.S455 (ebook) | LCC PZ7.7.S455 Fo 2018 (print) | DDC 741.5/973–dc23

LC record available at https://lccn.loc.gov/2017044293

Manufactured in the United States of America
1-39658-21287-2/27/2018

WHO'S WHO

Quillan Lu Hedgeson
aka: Q

Ray Ratzberg

Mr. Shrew
Media Specialist

Ms. Boar
Classroom Teacher

Mr. Teecher
Gym Teacher

Gloria Gopher
Elm Tree Park Guide

Satin

Officer Rocco

Oh! I should have spotted your bow tie camera. I like your new disguise.

This isn't a disguise! It's my new baseball cap and jersey.

For our field trip to Elm Tree Park? Sure, it's Opening Day. But aren't you taking things a bit far?

No, Ray! They're part of my uniform! I joined a baseball team.

I want to be just like Dormouse Sams. She's my favorite player.

Never heard of her.

She played a long time ago! In the past, there was a girls' pro league.

CHAPTER THREE
Pen Lifts and Ink Blots

Fake signatures often look shaky. That's because forgers press hard to get them just right.

Ray Ratzberg

I get it! I love the decls. Like this one: I smell stinky cheese and onions. But also something new!

Indeed! I'm trying a new Yumwich. The usual Limburger and onion, plus pineapple!

And? How is it?

?

Sometimes you shouldn't mess with the real deal.

CHAPTER FOUR
Dormouse Sams

At Elm Tree Park...

ELM TREE PARK

HOME OF THE METEORS

GO METEORS!

Ooh! I've never been to Opening Day! I hope the Meteors win!

I'm Gloria. Today you're in for a treat! I'm going to show you some sports history. Then we'll all watch the game.

Yippee! Yay! Woo-hoo!

Students, why doncha be quiet?!

Weeeee! Weeeee!

Settle down, Mr. Teecher. Settle.

Elm Tree Park has been around for eighty years. First, the early leagues came. And now the Elm Tree Meteors!

CHAPTER SIX

Time to Investigate

Feel free to look around, students!

Psst...are you sure this is **the** baseball?

It better be!

I only take it out for school visits. Your teachers called ahead and asked to see it.

And you are?

Quillan Lu Hedgeson! And I don't think this is the record-breaking ball.

Look at the shaky writing.

And the ink blots.

Oh no!

That...doesn't look quite right!

Plus the ball doesn't look old enough! My goodness!

I'm calling the police!

In the meantime, Q and I will inspect the scene.

Fifteen minutes later...

Q? Is that you? Nice getup! Are you in disguise again?

No! I joined a team!

I swing a hot bat myself. Any clues here?

Not yet.

Why are you here?

Someone stole a baseball.

Not the *Sams* ball??

You got it. Can I check your bag?

I *guess* so.

27

Officer Rocco continues her investigation...

...And the rest of the class leaves to watch the game.
But Q and Ray stay behind to look for clues.

Ugh! I should've kept my eye on the Sams ball.

Me too. Is it worth a lot of bread?

Yes! Which is probably why it's been stolen.

Unless a fan stole the ball just to keep it.

Ms. Boar is a fan, but the ball wasn't in her bag.

The guide could've switched the balls during our trip.

Or it could've been stolen before we arrived.

Wait a minute!

It's a start.

Speaking of starts, start heading to the game or you'll miss it. Let me know if something turns up.

CHAPTER SEVEN

Collecting Clues

Wednesday, outside Ms. Boar's classroom...

If we found Ms. Boar's pin, she's a suspect.

Maybe more clues came up during the start of the game.

Let's interview a student.

Super idea, sleuth! How about Satin? She's on my baseball team.

Let's look at some photos.

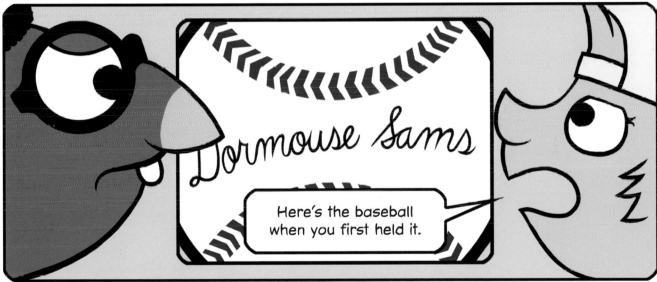

Here's the baseball when you first held it.

And here's the ball after everyone in the class passed it around.

BEFORE   **AFTER**

The paw-writing! It's different! See? Look close.

At Mr. Teecher's office...

Knock! Knock!

By gum! What brings you here?

We're investigating.

Oh, that's right. You two call yourselves detectives.

Sleuths, actually.

I would add: super sleuths!

Why did you ask to see the Sams baseball?

Can't remember if I did. We set up these field trips so far in advance. Have a look around.

CHAPTER EIGHT

Evidence

Back in the Secret Lab...

The baseball is **still** missing! I feel like I'm letting down Dormouse Sams.

But Sams would be proud of you! Think of all your baseball skills.

Oh, I don't know...

That's it!

Whenever Sams's team was about to lose, she mixed it up.

She'd fire off a new type of pitch!

So how do **we** mix it up?

Let's start by looking at our photos again.

Here's Ms. Boar with the baseball.

Hold on. Let me zoom in!

Isn't that... Mr. Teecher?

Nice hair! Did he just wake up?

On the school field...

Aren't you supposed to be in class?

Can I see your cap?

Not a good idea. My hair's a mess.

Take off the cap, Jim.

Happy?

When Mr. Teecher tried to forge the writing on the newer ball, he lifted the pen. It made blots. Plus his fake writing was shaky.

Dormouse Sams

During the tour, Mr. Teecher removed his hat.

But after the baseball went missing, he **wouldn't** remove it.

The ball had to be in his hat!

But why did Jim do it?

The money. He wasn't even a fan of Sams!

Because of him, we missed the opening pitch. And on Opening Day!

You're going to have a second chance! They want you to throw the opening pitch at the next Meteors game.

Nuts and berries!

And Ray, would you like to introduce Q to the fans?

You mean, on the microphone?

45

Elm Tree Park. One week later.

Fans, you're in for a treat!

Today you'll see the youngest pitcher ever to throw the opening pitch.

This is her first time on this mound. But it won't be her last.

Please give a big welcome to Quillan Lu **HEDGESON!**

WOOO! HOO! Yippee!

WHOOSSSSSSH!

Folks, she just fired a heater down the middle of the plate!

Ten minutes later...

There's our ace!

Wowza! Just *wowza!*

Aren't you going to tell Ray to settle down, Ms. Boar?

Not today! I'm very proud of you, Q! You too, Ray!

Besides, this isn't a school day. *Go Meteors!*

And *go Ray!* You did a *super* job of announcing my pitch!

I learned it all from you!

And you two make a top-notch *team!*

I'd say! We go together like Limburger and onions!

Or nuts and berries.

ABOUT THE AUTHOR

Trisha Speed Shaskan has written more than forty books for children, including the Q & Ray series and *Punk Skunks*, both of which are illustrated by her husband, Stephen Shaskan. As a child, Trisha played baseball at the park and softball on a team. Trisha and Stephen live in Minneapolis, Minnesota, with their cat, Eartha, and dog, Bea. Visit her at trishaspeedshaskan.com.

ABOUT THE ILLUSTRATOR

Stephen Shaskan is the author and illustrator of the picture books *A Dog Is a Dog*, *Big Choo*, *Max Speed*, *Toad on the Road: A Cautionary Tale*, *Toad on the Road: Mama and Me*, and *The Three Triceratops Tuff*. He's also the illustrator of *Punks Skunks*. Stephen is super excited to be creating the Q & Ray graphic novel series, since he grew up collecting, reading, and drawing comic books. Visit him at stephenshaskan.com.

FUN FACTS

In 1942 many young men in the United States were drafted to serve in World War II. People involved with baseball began to worry about the sport. With the young men away at war, baseball teams were short on players. Baseball parks were in danger of closing. And so a group of businesspeople created the All-American Girls Professional Baseball League (AAGPBL). This league operated from 1943 to 1954. During that time, more than six hundred women played professional baseball.

One of the best players in the AAGPBL was Doris Sams. For seven years, Doris Sams played for the Lassies. This team was based in Muskegon, Michigan, and later Kalamazoo, Michigan. She was the only player to be named to the AAGPBL all-star team as both a pitcher and outfielder. During the 1952 season, Sams set a record by hitting twelve home runs. She inspired the character Dormouse Sams too!